Beauty and the Beast

Belle to the Rescue

By Kitty Richards

Illustrated by the Disney Storybook Art Team

A GOLDEN BOOK • NEW YORK

randomhousekids.com
ISBN 978-0-7364-3915-2
Printed in the United States of America
10 9 8 7 6 5 4 3 2 1

One afternoon, Belle walked into the kitchen with a bag of clothing. "Mrs. Potts!" she called. "I found this in the foyer."

Mrs. Potts sighed. "The master asked me to get rid of his clothes," she explained. "They don't fit him anymore. Luckily, the peddler is coming today. He'll take them for us."

Belle put the bag back in the foyer, then heard
Chip calling her.

"Belle! Would you like to play hide-and-seek
with me?" he asked.

"I would love to," said Belle. She closed her eyes
and counted to twenty. "Ready or not, here I come!"
she called.

Just then, there was a knock on the door.

The peddler had arrived with his cart full of goods.

"We don't need anything today," said Belle, "but we do have something for you." She handed him the bag of clothing.

"Thank you!" exclaimed the peddler. He handed Belle a pair of ice skates. "I insist you take these in return. Goodbye!"

When the peddler had left, Belle started looking for Chip. She looked in the den.

She searched the bookshelves.

She even looked inside the suits of armor in the great hall. But Chip was nowhere to be found.

Belle was worried. She went to Lumiere for help.
"I haven't seen Chip since the peddler was here,"
she said. "Oh, no! He must have been hiding in the
bag of clothes I gave away!"

"We have to go get him before he's lost forever!"
Belle put on her cape and boots, then grabbed her
new ice skates, just in case.

Belle and Lumiere rode Philippe into the woods. Before long, the friends found the tracks the peddler's wagon had left in the snow.

"He went that way!" said Lumiere.

"If we hurry, we can catch up to him," said Belle.

Nearby, a little red bird watched the friends. She had taken a piece of ribbon from the peddler's cart for her nest. She wanted to help.

Philippe was galloping after the tracks, when suddenly—
Awooooooo! A wolf howled!

Philippe reared back and stumbled off the road into
a huge snowbank. Belle and Lumiere went flying!

Belle pulled herself and Lumiere out of the snow. Then she dug
Philippe out with one of her skates.

A few moments later, they were back on the peddler's trail—until the tracks disappeared in the new-fallen snow. "Which way should we go?" asked Lumiere. The red bird knew!

The bird flittered to a nearby tree, where Belle finally noticed her. Belle climbed up to the bird and spotted the peddler in the distance.

"He's across the lake!" she called to her friends. "Thank you," she added to the bird.

With the bird's help, Belle led her friends
to the lake. They could see the peddler on the
other side, heading away. They had to hurry!

Belle tried to cross the frozen lake on Philippe,
but the ice began to crack.
"Philippe is too heavy!" cried Lumiere.

Belle had an idea. "My ice skates!" She strapped them on and was soon gliding swiftly over the ice, the little red bird flying at her side.

Belle didn't notice the log in her path until it was almost too late.

Luckily, she swerved out of the way just in time!

Finally, Belle reached the peddler.
"Monsieur!" she called. "I think a very special
teacup fell into the bag of clothes I gave you. It's
small, with a chip on its rim."

"You went to all that trouble for a teacup with
a chip in it?" asked the peddler.

"It's my favorite one!" said Belle. She opened the bag and found Chip safely inside.

"I bet you thought you'd never find me in this hiding spot," said Chip with a grin.

"I'm so glad I did!" said Belle.